LEARN ABOUT VOLCANOES

by Golriz Golkar

Published by The Child's World®
1980 Lookout Drive • Mankato, MN 56003-1705
800-599-READ • www.childsworld.com

Design Elements: Shutterstock Images
Photographs ©: Shutterstock Images, cover (volcano), cover (jar), 1 (volcano), 1 (jar), 4 (oil), 4 (salt), 10, 14, 17, 19, 23; RT Images/Shutterstock Images, 4 (jar); Rick Orndorf, 5; Alan Budman/Shutterstock Images, 6; iStockphoto, 9, 20; Luka Kikina/Shutterstock Images, 13

Copyright © 2020 by The Child's World®
All rights reserved. No part of this book may be reproduced or utilized in any form or by any means without written permission from the publisher.

ISBN 9781503832169
LCCN 2018963091

Printed in the United States of America
PA02420

About the Author

Golriz Golkar is a teacher and children's author who lives in Nice, France. She enjoys cooking, traveling, and looking for ladybugs on nature walks.

TABLE OF CONTENTS

CHAPTER 1
Let's Make a Volcano! . . . 4

CHAPTER 2
What Is a Volcano? . . . 8

CHAPTER 3
What Causes a Volcanic Eruption? . . . 12

CHAPTER 4
What Happens after a Volcanic Eruption? . . . 18

Glossary . . . 22
To Learn More . . . 23
Index . . . 24

CHAPTER 1

Let's Make a Volcano!

MATERIALS
- ☐ Glass jar
- ☐ Water
- ☐ 1/3 cup vegetable oil
- ☐ Salt

It is a good idea to gather your materials before you begin.

After the oil sinks, it will rise back up like the hot rock and gas inside of a volcano.

STEPS

1. Pour 4 inches (10 cm) of water into the jar.

2. Add the oil. It will float above the water.

3. Shake one teaspoon of salt over the oil.

Volcanoes can be very dangerous. It is important to follow directions when near one to stay safe.

4. Watch the salt sink. Some oil will float down. The salt will dissolve in the water. The oil will rise to the top. This creates a **lava** effect.

5. Add more salt. This makes the oil float up and down. Your pretend lava will keep flowing.

CHAPTER 2

What Is a Volcano?

A volcano is an opening in Earth's crust. Volcanoes can **erupt**. During an eruption, gases, ash, and hot liquid rock called **magma** escape. Volcanoes are found on every continent. They even exist underwater.

During eruptions, volcanoes can release molten rock.

Most volcanoes do not constantly erupt. They look like regular mountains until an eruption begins.

The United States has several **active** volcanoes. Most are found in Alaska, Hawaii, and California. They erupt from time to time.

Dormant volcanoes are mostly inactive. They have not erupted in thousands of years. They might become active again. **Extinct** volcanoes are unlikely to erupt again.

The experiment shows a volcanic eruption. Adding salt creates pressure. It forces the oil down and up again. This makes a lava effect.

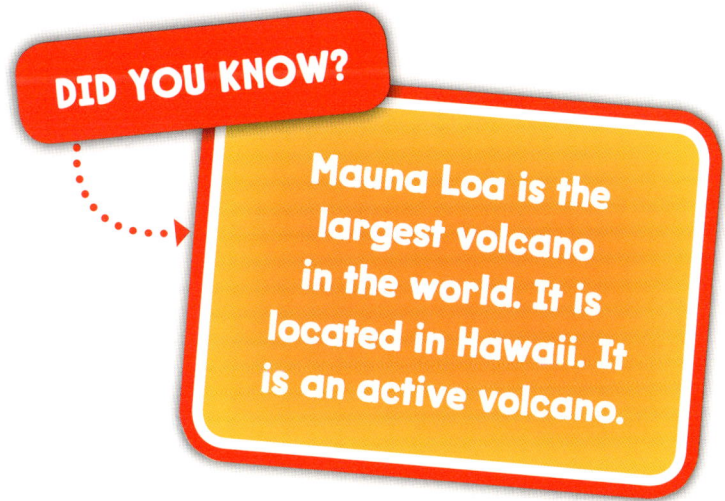

DID YOU KNOW?

Mauna Loa is the largest volcano in the world. It is located in Hawaii. It is an active volcano.

CHAPTER 3

What Causes a Volcanic Eruption?

Earth's crust contains large slabs of rock. They are called **tectonic plates**. Some plates are larger than continents. They rest above a layer of magma.

Tectonic plates shift often. They move closer together or farther apart. They move past each other. This creates pressure in the crust. Lots of pressure causes earthquakes.

Active volcanoes release smoke and ash before an eruption.

The movement of tectonic plates can cause earthquakes or volcanic eruptions.

The moving plates make changes in the magma. The movement can add new rocks or gases to the magma. This can change the temperature. Magma can flow to different places when plates move. The magma travels through cracks in the crust. It pushes up to the surface. Gases and ash rise with it. This is what makes the volcano erupt.

There are several types of volcanoes. Each kind erupts differently. Magma explodes from some volcanoes. It flows out gently from others. When magma reaches Earth's surface, it is called lava.

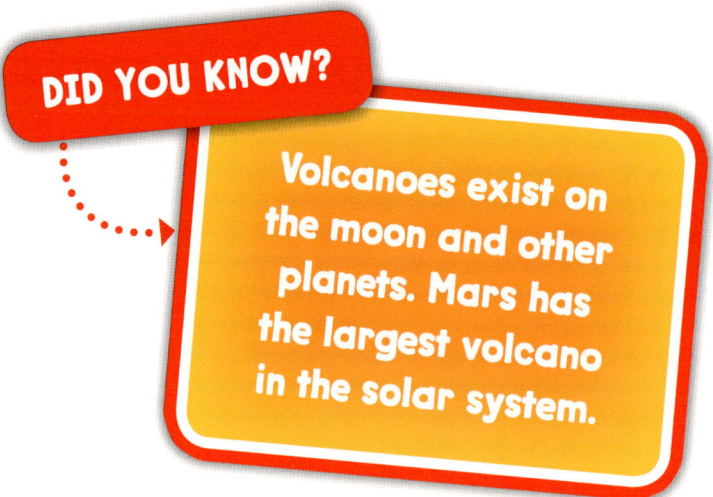

DID YOU KNOW?

Volcanoes exist on the moon and other planets. Mars has the largest volcano in the solar system.

Sometimes lava is very liquid and flows quickly. Other times lava is very thick and flows slowly.

CHAPTER 4

What Happens after a Volcanic Eruption?

Eruptions are very dangerous. Lava burns everything it touches. Lava can flow quickly. It travels up to 100 miles (160 km) per hour. If there is snow on the volcano, it melts rapidly. This causes mud flows. The mud can bury towns below.

Ash can travel far both before and after an eruption. It causes air and water pollution. People may have trouble breathing or seeing.

Volcanologists need special safety gear to protect them from hot lava.

Volcanologists study volcanoes that have erupted. They track earthquakes that occur below volcanoes. They study the gases that are released. They try to predict future eruptions. They hope to warn people when an eruption might happen.

Many people like to farm near volcanoes. Cooled lava slowly becomes a soil full of nutrients.

Lava and ash create nutrients in soil after an eruption. Nutrients help crops grow well. A volcano's heat and magma also provide energy. The magma can heat underground water. The hot water is sometimes used to create electricity.

DID YOU KNOW?

The Ring of Fire is a belt of land in the Pacific Ocean. It stretches for approximately 25,000 miles (40,000 km). Most of the world's volcanic eruptions occur here.

Glossary

active (ak-TIV) Active volcanoes are volcanoes that will likely erupt. Active volcanoes are most common in the Ring of Fire.

dormant (DOR-ment) Dormant volcanoes are inactive or at rest. A dormant volcano is one that has not erupted for many years.

erupt (ee-RUPT) To erupt is to burst forth and eject matter. A volcano will erupt lava, gases, and ash.

extinct (ex-TINKT) A volcano that is extinct is no longer active or existing. An extinct volcano is expected to never erupt again.

lava (LAH-vuh) Lava is magma that erupts from a volcano and reaches Earth's surface. Flowing lava can destroy anything in its path due to its intense heat.

magma (MAG-muh) Magma is hot melted rock beneath Earth's crust. Magma flows underground and becomes lava when it reaches the surface.

tectonic plates (tek-TON-ik PLAYTS) Tectonic plates are large rock segments in Earth's crust that move in relation to each other. The shifting of tectonic plates can cause earthquakes and volcanic eruptions.

volcanologist (vul-ka-NAWL-o-jist) A volcanologist is a person who studies volcanoes. A volcanologist studies a volcano's eruption history and predicts when the next eruption may occur.

To Learn More

In the Library

Ganeri, Anita. *Eruption! The Story of Volcanoes.*
New York, NY: DK Children, 2015.

Matthas, Seth. *How Do Volcanoes Explode?*
New York, NY: PowerKids Press, 2018.

York, M. J. *Igneous Rocks.* Mankato,
MN: The Child's World, 2017.

On the Web

Visit our website for links about volcanoes:
childsworld.com/links

Note to Parents, Teachers, and Librarians: We routinely verify our Web links to make sure they are safe and active sites. So encourage your readers to check them out!

Index

active, 10-11
ash, 8, 15, 18, 21

continent, 8, 12

dormant, 11

earthquake, 12, 19
electricity, 21
erupt, 8-11, 15-16, 18-19
extinct, 11

gas, 8, 15, 19

lava, 7, 11, 16, 18, 21

magma, 8, 12, 15-16, 21
mud flow, 18

tectonic plates, 12-15

volcanologist, 19